GRuBtoWN taLes
Book Three

The FaR FRoM GReat Escape

or

The Light, the Switch
and the Wardrobe

A bit about the author

Philip Ardagh is the award-winning author of the Eddie Dickens adventures, currently in over 30 languages. He wrote BBC radio's first truly interactive radio drama, collaborated with Sir Paul McCartney on his first children's book and is a 'regularly irregular' reviewer of children's books for the *Guardian*. Married with a son, he divides his time between Tunbridge Wells and Grubtown, where he cultivates his impressive beard.

GRuBtoWN taLes
Book Three

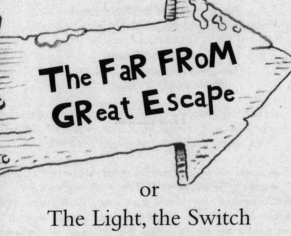

The FaR FRoM
GReat Escape

or
The Light, the Switch
and the Wardrobe

by Philip Ardagh
Illustrated by Jim Paillot

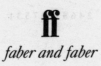

faber and faber

First published in 2009
by Faber and Faber Limited
Bloomsbury House, 74–77 Great Russell Street,
London WC1B 3DA

Typeset by Faber and Faber Limited
Printed in England by CPI BookMarque, Croydon

A CIP record for this book
is available from the British Library

A bit about Grubtown

You won't find Grubtown on any maps. The last time any map-makers were sent anywhere near the place they were found a week later wearing nothing but pages from a telephone directory, and calling for their mothers. It's certainly a town and certainly grubby – except for the squeaky-clean parts – but everything else we know about the place comes from Beardy Ardagh, town resident and author of these tales.

Grubtown TaLes were made possible through the participation of the following people, animals and organisations:

THE GRUBTOWN
CHAMBER OF COMMERCE

THE GRUBTOWN
CHAMBER OF
HORRORS

THE OFFICE
*of the Mayor
of Grubtown*

OFFAL'S
SUNBEDS

THE SHED
*of the Mayor
of Grubtown*

*The Mayor
of Grubtown
Himself*

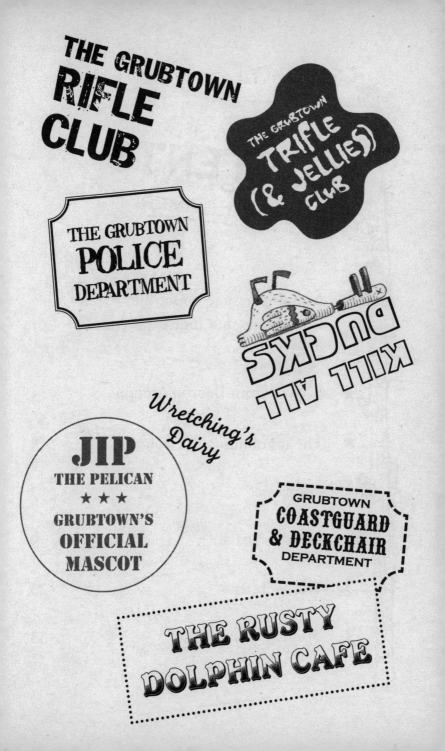

CONTENTS

A short message about the illustrations that didn't quite make it into this book

Grubtown is very fortunate to be the home of the well-known artist Partial Coggs. When he found out that fellow Grubtown citizen, Beardy Ardagh, was writing about events which have happened in the town, he got very excited. He not only got excited, he also got in his car and drove straight over to Beardy Ardagh's house. On the seat next to him were a number of sketches of key Grubtown inhabitants . . . because Partial Coggs wanted to draw the pictures for this latest book. Beardy Ardagh, however, was – and still is – very happy with Jim who has already drawn the pictures for the other books and told Mr Coggs so. To cut a long story short, Mr Coggs burst into tears and locked himself in the downstairs loo. And he is still in the loo at the time this explanation was written. Oh dear.

A word from
Beardy Ardagh

Y^{erch!}

Grubtown

3

The inhabitants
of Grubtown

At the back of the book (starting on page 127), you'll find a list of some of the people who live in Grubtown, including Jilly Cheeter, Mango Claptrap *and* Partial Coggs in the hope that, on hearing this news, he might STOP SULKING AND COME OUT OF THE DOWNSTAIRS LOO. Not all of the people in this book appear in this list and not all of people in this list appear in this book. Is that clear? We do hope so.

Postscript

If you have a script, you're welcome to post it. But not to me. If you don't get this joke, that's not my problem either.

Beardy Ardagh

Grubtown

Chapter One
Disaster Strikes!

A lighthouse without a light is just a dark house, and a dark house isn't much good at doing a lighthouse's job (which is to stay bright to warn ships to steer clear of land). It's a bit like having a cake factory without cakes, but more dangerous for ships.

Here in Grubtown we've always been very proud of our lighthouse or, to be more accurate, the lighthouse's light bulb. Not only is it likely to be the **BIGGEST** light bulb we'll ever see, but it's also incredibly old. Then, one night, it finally went 'ping' and stopped working. It's still ridiculously big for a light bulb and it's still ridiculously *old* for a light bulb but somehow it's not as exciting now that it doesn't work.

Most of us townsfolk will never forget the night that the lighthouse light finally went out. Garlic Hamper, our lighthouse keeper for the past thirty-three years, was sitting in his circular living-room in the lighthouse when it happened.

For about

as long as anyone can remember, Garlic has been making a model of Grubtown out of matchsticks. He was just about to add another stick to the roof of Purple Outing's recently repaired Music Shack when he heard the 'ping' and instantly noticed that the beam of light that should have been sweeping past his tiny window wasn't (sweeping past his tiny window). Instead, outside was as dark as a black bat with its eyes closed.

The rest of the lights in the light-house were working fine, though, so Garlic had no trouble finding his way up into the lantern room which housed the bulb and the great big lenses which beamed the light into the night. Only now, of course, the lenses weren't doing anything.

In case there was just a loose connection stopping the flow of electricity from reaching the bulb, Garlic Hamper gave the whole thing a swift kick with one of his official lighthouse-keeper's standard-issue black lace-up boots. (This had worked in the past.) But he had heard the dreaded 'ping' and, deep down in the brainiest part of his brain, knew what it must mean.

This was an emergency. But what should he do?

Panic?

Close his eyes and pretend it never happened?

Hope that if he did nothing things would somehow put themselves right?

Garlic Hamper thought fast and he thought well.

QUESTION: Who do people usually call in an emergency?

ANSWER: The fire, police, ambulance or coastguard services.

QUESTION: And what do a fire engine, ambulance, police car and coastguard's vehicles have in common?

ANSWER: LIGHTS . . . FLASHING . . . ON TOP.

Like a lighthouse has!

If he could get ALL of the emergency services to come as fast as possible, he could have them line up their vehicles on the waterfront with lights flashing. That way, at least, any passing ships might see something to warn them they were near land. Ships such as that great big one that was heading *right his way*. (Garlic planned to send out an emergency all-frequencies radio message too.)

He cranked a large handle to his right which set off a siren which wailed like an injured whale moaning through a megaphone. This would be heard right out to sea as well as summoning help. Next, he –

CRUNCH!!!

Too late.

That great big ship had just hit something very solid indeed.

It was certainly a night I won't forget in a hurry. I was one of the Grubtown citizens who was enjoying the 'Hot Chocolate and Bubble-Wrap-Popping Night' at **THE RUSTY DOLPHIN**, as the ship – which turned out to be called *The Plucked Grape* – ploughed up the beach towards it.

When Garlic Hamper's siren started its terrifying whaley wail, Chevvy Offal (of Offals's Sunbeds) shouted, 'Run for your lives!' dropping a large sheet of almost-completely-popped bubble-wrap to the floor, and dashing for the door.

'Stay calm, everyone!' shouted The Rusty Dolphin's owner, Camshaft Thrift, above the noise. 'Don't panic!' His words might have sounded better if he hadn't been elbowing his way past his customers as he spoke them. He had the cash register under his arm.

The mayor's brother, Hacking-Cough Gomez (who'd been enjoying a hot chocolate with extra marshmallows and whipped cream topping) started coughing frantically. Fellow Grubtown citizen, Mrs Awning, who

was sitting at the next table, tried slapping him across the back – in case he was choking – but missed. Instead she hit her wrist against one of the cafe's wooden pillars, so ended up being one of the few people injured that night. (On the way to hospital later, she fell out of the back of the ambulance when it swerved to avoid a duck, and ended up with a badly grazed elbow.)

The music for the bubble-wrap evening was being provided by the Grumbly girls, seven charming girls whose voices sound surprisingly like the lighthouse siren. In fact, when the siren first started, I'm sure I wasn't alone in thinking that this was a new chorus to one of their songs. Later, of course, they wrote a song to commemorate the whole experience. (They always do that kind of thing.) It was called, '**We Nearly Got Hit By A Ship, But That Didn't Stop Us From Singing**'. When, some months later, the song title appeared on one of their posters, someone wrote underneath it: **WHICH IS A SHAME** (and there's no way you can prove that it was me).

I made it out of the cafe just in time to see the front – the hull? – of an enormous ship loom out of the darkness and bulldoze its way up the short distance of beach and into **THE RUSTY DOLPHIN** with that terrifying

CRUNCH!!! sound

I mentioned earlier.

The cafe was destroyed as easily as one of Garlic Hamper's matchstick models would be if I was to step on it (which, I must confess, I've done by mistake in the past).

The noise was so loud that it travelled far inland and even through the (very thick) walls of Grubtown Jail, reaching the ears of the handful of prisoners inside.

Very few people get locked up in Grubtown because Mayor Flabby Gomez would rather convicted criminals spend their own money on feeding, cleaning and keeping themselves warm, than the town having to do it for them. (He likes to use the town's money for more important things, such as the Mayor's Emergency Cake Fund.) There were eight prisoners inside the jail at the time, which was a lot by Grubtown standards.

A long-time inmate was a chap called Mickey 'Steamroller' Johnson who'd done some wild and dangerous things with his steamroller in the past. Just about everyone – including me – feels a lot safer knowing that he's safely behind bars and hopes that he's not going to be released sometime soon. (I like to be able to wander down to the newsagent's to buy a copy of **BIG BEARDS WEEKLY**, or some straw for the troll in my airing cupboard, without the fear of ending up as flat as a pancake.)

Another prison regular is Hobo Browne, and he was in jail on the day of the mighty crunch. Hobo is either a smelly tramp, a gentleman of the road, or a homeless person, depending on your point of view. Whatever he is, he's also a nice bloke and Constable Gelatine had kindly had him locked up (again) for a few days, so that he could have a comfy bed and some cooked meals for a few days.

This left six other prisoners. And these six

other weren't in the slightest bit interested in the noise they'd just heard. Why not? Because these six prisoners were far more interested in themselves. And they were making BIG plans.

Chapter Two
The Flabster

Flabby Gomez tried ordering a new bulb for the lighthouse off the Internet but it seemed that they'd stopped making ones like that in 1908. Instead, he ordered the Grubtown Maintenance Department to rewire the lighthouse so that it would be lit by lots of ordinary-sized light bulbs (which wouldn't all go 'ping' at once).

Unfortunately, the Grubtown Maintenance Department is scared of heights so asked Furl Claptrap to do it. (The Grubtown Maintenance Department is the mayor's brother, Hacking-Cough Gomez.)

Furl Claptrap is good at being *bad* at just about anything and everything you can do with your hands.

He can build a wall.

Badly.

He can 'fix' a boiler.

Badly.

Lay paving slabs; trim hedges; plumb in washing machines; make shadow puppets.

Badly; badly; badly; *badly*.

He can take just about anything to pieces and put it back together again with at least two – usually important – bits left over.

But he's a hard-worker, cheap and owed Hacking-Cough a favour. So he agreed to go to the lighthouse.

Furl's elder son, Vestige Claptrap, wasn't interested in helping his dad. He was more interested in throwing stones at *The Plucked Grape* which was still stuck on the beach. He usually throws stones at the signs along the shore, so the ship must have made a nice change for him. (And a bigger target too, of course.)

Vestige Claptrap's favourite targets are the signs which read:

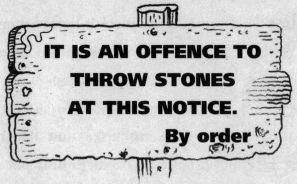

IT IS AN OFFENCE TO
THROW STONES
AT THIS NOTICE.
By order

Little does he know that they were
deliberately put there to encourage stone-
throwing idiots to do just that rather than:

    (A) throw stones at seagulls (which
          isn't nice for the birds); or

    (B) throw stones at old bottles (which
          may break and later cut swimmers'
          feet).

Our chief of police, Grabby Hanson, put
those signs up. He's clever like that, even
though he's forever taking people's stuff
without asking. (By the time he was five
years old, he'd grabbed everything from
biscuits off plates and wigs off bald men to
slates off the roof of Leaky Hall, which used

26

to be called something different before then.)

Vestige Claptrap may have been more interested in stone-throwing than helping out his dad in the lighthouse, but his younger brother Mango was really excited by the idea. He'd never been inside the lighthouse. It was strictly 'out of bounds'. Someone who was as excited as Mango Claptrap about exploring the lighthouse was his best friend Jilly Cheeter.

On the day that Jilly Cheeter and Mango Claptrap first went to the lighthouse, Flabby Gomez wasn't having a good morning. Since the Grubtown mayor's official residence had been destroyed during **THE WORLD BEATERS' FESTIVAL** a few years earlier, he'd been living with his family in a garden shed.

This was no ordinary shed, though. You couldn't expect the mayor to live in a

common-or-garden (garden) shed.

No.

This was a mighty big shed. It was eight storeys high, but the Gomez family only lived on six floors. They used the seventh for storage and the eighth was inhabited by a group of escaped lab rats (who, amongst other things, loved listening to most classical music). The shed was only meant to be a temporary home, while Flabby was knitting a new one. And that morning he had run out of wool.

'I'm never going to get our new house finished at this rate,' he sighed over a pile of second-hand pancakes.

'Don't worry, Flabster,' said his wife, Pritt, giving him an affectionate kiss on the forehead. 'I'm sure it'll have been well worth waiting for when it's finally finished.'

'And, until then, we're stuck in this dump,' grumbled Tundra, with a mouth full of crispy bacon. Unfortunately for Flabby and Pritt Gomez, he is their son and heir.

'If you don't like it, Tundra, you could always find your own place to live,' said Pritt. (She didn't mean it. Tundra was too young for that, though I can't remember exactly how old he was at the time.)

'There aren't any jobs,' Tundra muttered.

Flabby snorted like a pig who didn't believe what he'd just heard. (You know the

29

sound.) 'Aren't any jobs for a Gomez in Grubtown!?' he said in amazement. 'I own Grubtown, Tundra! If you go down to Rambo Sanskrit's office tomorrow, I'll have him make you Fire Chief.'

Rambo Sanskrit is the council's official job-giver-outer. (He has a very special badge to prove it.)

'Dad,' moaned Tundra, 'I meant a *proper* job.'

'It is a proper job. You can order people into burning buildings and have fun with hoses,' said the mayor. 'You can even ride in any of the fire engines whenever you want, with the siren going and everything.'

'But I'm only a kid, Dad. I want a kid's job. One which I can do properly and where people will take me seriously.' This might have seemed more impressive if Tundra wasn't dressed – as always – as a cowboy and (still) talking with his mouth full.

'What about being the next duck-gatherer?' suggested his mother. She turned to Flabby. 'You're always saying that the people who replaced that Cheeter girl are no good.'

It's the job of the Grubtown duck-gatherer to round up all the town's ducks at night and keep them in the custom-built duck house (which cost millions), and then to shoo them all out again early the following morning. The main reason for this is the Fox family. I won't say more here other than that they own a shop called KILL ALL DUCKS, which should give you a clue to their feelings about quacking water fowl. They had also fairly recently been sent to prison for doing something unspeakable.

There are six of them.

One, two, three, four, five, six.

'I'm not getting up at the crack of dawn to shovel duck poo!' Tundra protested, before reaching across for another podgy-fingered

handful of crispy bacon.

'Then quit complaining about living here,' said Pritt Gomez.

Though Pritt Gomez is pencil-thin and carries a pencil to prove it (or maybe she uses it to write with), Tundra takes after his father who, in turn, takes after his father, Big Man

Gomez (who'd owned Grubtown before Flabby).

One day, to everyone's surprise, Big Man Gomez had held a raffle of all his possessions. Flabby had won Grubtown, which most people were very pleased about. Particularly Flabby.

Then, a week later, Big Man Gomez had died. (Which people were even more pleased about.) Nowadays, Flabby keeps his father's ashes in a large coffee tin on a shelf. Big Man Gomez always loved drinking coffee (especially when someone else was paying).

'I'm going out to order some more wool,' said Flabby, who'd been up much of the night knitting the fourth bedroom. 'Just as soon as I've eaten the rest of these pancakes.'

He was about to put another forkful to his mouth when the house phone rang. He answered it with a: 'Yup?'

'*Mayor Gomez?*' said a voice, strained

through an old sock.

'Yes,' said Flabby.

'*I have a tip-off*,' said the sock–muffled voice.

'A tip-off?' said Flabby. 'Who is this?'

'*Just listen*,' said the voice. '*There's going to be a jailbreak, and I'll tell you who, I'll tell you where and I'll tell you when.*'

'I'm listening,' said Flabby Gomez.

Chapter Three
Bright Ideas

A proper stone-built round-walled lighthouse with a big stone spiral staircase going up, up, up is an amazing place. There's something magical about it. Particularly if the outside is painted with thick red and white stripes like ours, as all good lighthouses should be. (Don't argue.)

Jilly Cheeter and Mango Claptrap were so excited to be allowed inside the lighthouse that Mango's dad let him unlock the door with the huge black iron key. There was an echo as Mango lifted the latch. They went inside.

They found themselves in a surprisingly large stone-floored (round) entrance hall with the base of the stairs straight ahead. There was an old metal light switch to the left of the stairs and an old wooden wardrobe built into the curved wall to the left of that. Hanging from a nail in the front of one of the wardrobe doors was a tide timetable. Taped to the door was a very old, very faded picture of a mermaid (probably not a photo). In front of the wardrobe were two enormous wellington boots, one green one black.

'Where's Garlic Hamper?' Mango asked, looking around.

'Mayor Gomez sent him off on holiday,' said his dad.

'Holiday?'

'Holiday.' His dad nodded. 'Flabby said there wasn't much point in a keeper keeping the lighthouse when there's no light in the lighthouse to keep lit.'

'He has a point, Mr Claptrap,' said Jilly Cheeter.

'It smells funny in here,' said Mango.

'Don't look at me,' said his dad.

'I wasn't,' said Mango.

'It smells damp,' said Jilly.

'Fishy,' said Mango.

'Damp *and* fishy,' said Jilly. '*And* smoky. A bit like Garlic Hamper.' She wondered whether the lighthouse smelled of the lighthouse keeper or the lighthouse keeper smelled of the lighthouse.

Just then, a door of the wardrobe swung open with a creak. Jilly Cheeter caught sight of a uniform before Mr Claptrap pushed it shut again.

'Do lighthouse keepers wear special

38

uniforms?' she asked.

'I've never seen old Garlic wearing one,' said Mango's dad.

'Whenever I've seen old Hamper around town, he's normally wearing his peaked cap and that blue fisherman's sweater with the holes in it,' said Mango.

'What about on Everyone-Parade-About-A-Bit Day?' asked Jilly Cheeter.

If Garlic Hamper was ever to wear a uniform, Everyone-Parade-About-A-Bit Day would be the day to do it. Everyone-Parade-About-A-Bit Day was one of Flabby Gomez's first bright ideas when he won the town in that raffle. He decreed that the eighth Monday in each year would be a public holiday in Grubtown and there would be parades like the townsfolk had never seen before. (Especially those townsfolk who had never seen a parade.)

Mayor Flabby Gomez not only had the

police, fire-fighters, nurses and paramedics parade in their uniforms but also had townsfolk appear in their traditional work clothes, from butchers in their striped aprons to the cinema doorman in his impressive blue and red uniform, to Grubtown's park-keepers brandishing their litter-picker-upper pointy-stick things.

Then there were children in costumes

depicting key moments in Grubtown's history, from the Theft of the Great Gizzard in 1628 to the Raising of the Flag over Large Lenny's in 1976. In later years (during her time as official duck-gatherer) Jilly Cheeter had been required to dress as a duck. (The duck-hating Fox family threw stale rock cakes at her.)

None of them remembered having seen

Garlic Hamper at the parades, let alone in a proper uniform.

'Why do you ask, Jilly?' said Furl Claptrap.

'No reason,' said Jilly. She'd sneak another peek at the uniform in the built-in wardrobe another time.

'This way,' said Furl Claptrap beginning the long climb up the winding stone stairs, his red metal toolbox in hand. He swung it as though it was as light as a handbag.

When they reached the first landing, they stopped to explore. There was a sitting-room and a kitchen. Both had curved-back furniture especially made to sit up against the circular walls.

'This is fantastic!' said Mango Claptrap.

'Awesome!' said Jilly Cheeter.

'Where are Garlic Hamper's matchstick models, Dad?' asked Mango.

'Sonia Pipkin's looking after them while he's away,' said Furl Claptrap. 'He was worried they might get damaged while the building work's going on.'

'Oh,' said Mango with a nod.

Sonia Pipkin is the best builder in Grubtown and I'm not just saying that because she's halfway through bricking-up the door to my guest bedroom and I don't want the job left half done. (No guest bedroom means I'll be bothered by fewer friends and relatives wanting to stay. 'Sorry,' I'll be able to say. 'No room!')

'Look at this!' said Jilly Cheeter. She was lifting the lid of an ancient-looking chest, the back part of which appeared to be built into the wall.

'Don't go nosing inside things, you two,' said Furl Claptrap. 'Remember that this is Mr Hamper's home as well as a lighthouse.'

They carried on up the stairs to the next level. This was Garlic Hamper's bedroom, and very cosy it was too. Again, it had specially made curved-back furniture to fit snugly against the round walls. There was another large wardrobe and a low chest of drawers.

There were even two curved pictures.

One was of a banana; the other, a boomerang.

To one side of the bed was a metal ladder set into the wall, reminding both Mango and Jilly of the ladder which Purple Outing had climbed down to discover Hybrid Byword's hoard. If you're not familiar with that particular tale, we'll pause while you hang your head in shame.

   . . . *Humm humm humm* . . .

   . . . *Dooby-dooby-doo* . . .

   . . . *Ooo! Ooo! Ooo!* . . .

   . . . *Hey ho* . . .

   . . . *Nonny-nonny-no* . . .

There. And apologies to those of you who were held up by gaps in other readers' knowledge. (It's embarrassing, isn't it?)

At the top of the ladder was a large – perfectly round – hole cut into the wooden ceiling.

'That's the only way up to the lantern room,' said Furl Claptrap. 'Part of my job is to get the old bulb all the way down and out of the lighthouse in one piece,' said Furl. 'The mayor wants to stick it in the museum. He reckons there are probably only a few left in the world.'

'I hope you don't drop it,' said Jilly.

'If you do, Dad,' said Mango Claptrap, 'you'll need a giant dustpan and brush.'

Furl Claptrap laughed, but he did look a little worried.

Speaking of worried, that's exactly what the prison guard at Grubtown Jail was feeling around about then too. Half an hour earlier he'd come back from letting Hobo Browne out of the front gate with the pockets of Hobo's shabby (and very smelly) overcoat filled with sandwiches, to find just one remaining prisoner in the cells instead of seven. Losing six prisoners wasn't the sort of thing a prison guard was supposed to let happen . . . but they must still be in the jail *somewhere*. He began searching the place from top to bottom, then bottom to top. Then top to bottom again. No wonder he had a bad feeling about this.

Chapter Four
An Odd Kind
of Warning

The view from the lantern room at the top of the lighthouse is amazing. You can see right across Grubtown. On a clear day, anyone with reasonable eyesight would be able to see as far as the rooftops of the village of Werty, with its crooked church-spire. You can see patches of green – including Brambly Park, Woody Wood and Really-Little-More–Than-A-Patch-Of-Grass-With-A-Big-Tree-In-It-Park – and the blue of Ah-Isn't-This-A-Lovely-Spot Lake and of the River

Flow, spanned by the new Flimsy Bridge.
(The old Flimsy Bridge had been too flimsy.)
On the outskirts of Grubtown, there's
Wretching's Dairy and the patch of scrub
land on which lies the abandoned turning-

handle of what was going to be the world's
largest pencil sharpener. You can see anything
and everything. Look from the other side and
you can see miles out to sea.

Look down in one particular direction and

you can see *The Crooked Sixpence*. For those of you who don't already know, I should explain that *The Crooked Sixpence* is an illegal gambling ship. It doesn't go anywhere but is permanently moored just off shore, beyond the jetties. The only way to reach it is by rowing boat or motor launch or, I suppose, swimming.

It's illegal because you're not allowed to gamble in this neck of the woods (or part of the water). Gambling is STRICTLY AGAINST THE LAW – let me repeat that: STRICTLY AGAINST THE LAW – and there's an end to it. Except that Flabby Gomez doesn't mind the ship being there because he owns it, and our chief of police, Grabby Hanson, doesn't mind it being there because his sister, Pageant Conquest, is in charge of all on-board refreshments: any profit made from selling food and drink goes into her pockets. Which means that everyone is perfectly happy about *The Crooked Sixpence* except for a handful of Grubtowners.

As it was morning, the floating casino was closed and Partial Coggs (Grubtown's resident artist) was aboard, deep in conversation with Purple Outing (a very rich man), and Carlo Monte (the famous riverboat gambler who now runs *The Crooked Sixpence* for the mayor). Coggs was arguing that the sky was, in fact, not blue. It was, he claimed, made up of a whole palette of different colours and we only said that it was blue because that's what teachers told us when we were little and, as grown-ups we were all too lazy to see for ourselves that this was, in fact, lies, lies, *lies*.

Partial Coggs got all hot and flustered and waved his arms around a lot when he was telling them this. (The truth be told, he was probably more than a little annoyed that Carlo Monte had just beaten him in a

double-or-quits game of *I'll Tickle Thomas*.)
He knocked over one of a number of sacks of
money that were lying around (which Carlo
Monte had yet to take to the bank), and even
foamed at the mouth a little. The whole thing
really seemed to matter to him. Artists can be
a bit like that when it comes to colours. (It's
like authors with book titles. My publishers
wanted to change the title of this one to

Twinkle-Toes the Very Pink and Very Sparkly Fairy Loves to Ride Lovely Unicorns because they thought it might sell more copies. I punched myself in the nose, saying that I would do it again if they didn't leave the title alone. That showed them!)

The discussion – okay: argument – was getting even more heated when the three men were interrupted by a polite cough. They all turned, to be confronted by Wide Brim Petty-Mandrake.

This was a shock. Wide Brim Petty-Mandrake is one of the handful of Grubtowners (I recently mentioned) who doesn't like *The Crooked Sixpence* being here. He is also one of the least-liked inhabitants of Grubtown. He's won that unofficial competition every year without even entering.

(One year, the dog-poo bin by the east entrance to Brambly Park was voted a more popular guest than he was in a list of guests for an imaginary tea party. Petty-Mandrake would have come bottom if the list hadn't included an escaped bear which had recently eaten a very popular scout master.)

Mr Petty-Mandrake is very slim, extremely good-looking and has perfect white teeth. Not a hair on his head is ever out of place. The lower half of his face is covered in perfect designer stubble and his clothes always look perfect. (I don't know about you, but I can never completely trust someone who walks around looking like a shop window dummy. It's not that I've ever thrown mud at him or anything – or, if I have, I wasn't the only one – but looking that perfect is just plain *wrong* somehow.)

Petty-Mandrake was one of the victims of a freak wind we had a few years back, when half a dozen or so townsfolk were blown great distances. (One Grubtown citizen, Mrs Awning, was actually found out at sea, clinging to a startled seal.) Petty-Mandrake was found stuck up a tree around the back of Marley Gripe's place. Police Chief Grabby Hanson, who'd been leading the search party, said that he looked as though he must have ironed and pressed his clothes up the tree while waiting to be rescued.

So just about everything about Wide Brim Petty-Mandrake's appear-

ance is very lovely indeed. But that's not why people hate him. His voice is like someone doing the silliest voice they can think of while talking into a shiny metal bucket. But that's not why most people hate him either.

The reason why this man is SO unpopular is that he complains (in his very silly voice). He complains even more than that whingeing Fox family before they were jailed, and that's saying something!

He once complained to the manager at the local garden centre that, if looked at from a certain angles, through half-closed eyes, the display of bird tables and bird feeders appeared to spell out a VERY rude word indeed.

In Chinese.

On yet ANOTHER occasion – *sigh* – he called the police when someone looked at him 'in a funny way'. That person had been Mrs Petty-Mandrake. She now lives in

Africa. Alone. And is, apparently, very happy.

And Wide Brim Petty-Mandrake had sworn never – EVER, EVER, EVER – to set foot aboard 'that floating house of badness' (which is what he calls *The Crooked Sixpence*).

But now here he was.

'I'm sorry to trouble you, gentlemen,' he said, 'but I was hoping to speak with Chief Hanson. I rang the police station and Constable Gelatine's nephew said that he'd be here.'

Monte, Coggs and Outing knew that Gelatine's sister's boy, Mustard Tripwire, wasn't the brightest firework in the sky, but none of them was going to admit this to the wildly unpopular Mr Petty-Mandrake.

'Well, if Officer Tripwire says that the chief is going to be here, then I've no doubt he'll be here soon,' said Carlo Monte.

'What's the problem, Mr Petty-Mandrake, if
you don't mind my asking?'

'The problem,' squeaked Wide Brim,
removing his hat to reveal an impressively
bumpy bump, 'is that the vile Fox family
bopped me over the head and stole my

hearse.' (Didn't I mention that Wide Brim Petty-Mandrake is Grubtown's only undertaker? Well, I have now.)

'But the Foxes are in prison!' Partial Coggs protested.

'Not any more they're not,' said Petty-Mandrake, rubbing his bump.

There was a dramatic piano chord.

'Sorry,' said Partial Coggs, who'd sat on the keyboard of the baby grand in the corner of the casino.

Chapter Five
Lookout

With the enormous light bulb now successfully out of the lantern, Furl Claptrap wanted to wrap it in bubble-wrap to protect it before trying to get it downstairs. He'd need plenty of it, which wouldn't have been a problem if there hadn't been the 'Hot Chocolate and Bubble-Wrap-Popping

Night' at **THE RUSTY DOLPHIN**. Of course, the event had been abandoned long before all the rolls of bubble-wrap had been used up, but these had been lost in the wreckage of the cafe. (Some of it was probably actually UNDER the ship stranded on the beach.)

'Any ideas what we could use instead?' asked Furl.

'Blankets?' suggested Mango.

'Duvets?' suggested Jilly Cheeter. 'They'd give even more padding.'

'Good idea,' said Furl Claptrap, 'though we'll have to tape a few together to cover the whole bulb. I'll nip back home and get some.'

Furl went out past the upturned clinker-built rowing boat and jumble of tangled old fishing nets, and jumped into his open-backed truck to drive home. He gave a lazy wave – more like swatting away a dozy fly

– and was off.

With Mango's father out of the way, Jilly Cheeter decided that now was an IDEAL opportunity to take a proper look at the *uniform* hanging up in the wardrobe downstairs. What did Garlic Hamper want with a uniform? Maybe she could find out what kind it was. Find out who would wear such a thing.

She reached the bottom of the spiral staircase and was just about to pull open the wardrobe door when there was *honk-honk-honking* of an unfamiliar car horn. Jilly crossed the stone-flagged floor and yanked open the front door. Mango Claptrap, meanwhile, hurtled himself downstairs (in those ridiculous shorts of his) and ended up at Jilly's side, both framed in the doorway.

They found Flabby Gomez squeezing out of his outsized car, now parked by the old fishing nets.

'Hello, Mr Mayor,' said Jilly Cheeter.

'Hello, Jilly,' said Flabby, probably wishing that his son, Tundra, was a bit more like her. (Clever. Enthusiastic. Polite. Not dressed as a cowboy.) 'Your father not here?' he asked Mango, who was panting for breath.

'Gone to find some duvets,' Mango Claptrap replied between gulps.

'To wrap the old bulb in,' explained Jilly Cheeter.

'Good thinking,' said Flabby Gomez, clearly impressed. He strode up to the lighthouse door. 'You must have a great view up there. You haven't seen anything strange, have you?'

'Strange, Mr Mayor?' asked Jilly Cheeter.

'Like what, Mr Mayor?' asked Mango Claptrap.

'Like the Fox family?' asked Flabby Gomez.

'They're certainly strange, Mr Mayor,' said

Jilly, 'but aren't they still in prison after that business with the –'

'They've escaped,' said Flabby.

'Wow!' said Mango Claptrap,

'Wow, indeed,' said the mayor. 'I had a tip-off but it wasn't quite accurate.'

'How do you mean, Mr Mayor?' asked Mango,

'Well, I was told that the jailbreak would be tomorrow, so I thought we had a little more time on our hands.'

'But instead the Foxes broke out today?' said Mango Claptrap.

'That's it,' nodded the mayor. He studied the boy in the funny shorts. 'As you know, Chief Grabby Hanson doesn't have enough manpower to throw up a cordon around the whole town,' he said, which was certainly true. At the time, the Grubtown Police Department was made up of Chief Kumquat 'Grabby' Hanson, Sergeant Constable Gelatine and

Gelatine's nephew Officer Mustard Tripwire. Maths isn't one of my strong points, but I reckon that made three. 'So we're going to have to enlist the eyes and ears of the good citizens of Grubtown.'

'And you think the lighthouse would make a good lookout tower?' said Mango excitedly.

'You might spot something,' Flabby nodded. 'And Garlic Hamper isn't here to quote coastguard rules and tell us why we can't.' He sniffed the air. 'This place smells

damp and fishy . . .' he said. He sniffed again. 'And even a little smoky.'

'Just like Garlic Hamper,' said Jilly and Mango.

'Just what I was thinking,' nodded Flabby Gomez. 'Oh well,' he said. 'Does either of you have a mobile phone?'

Jilly and Mango shook their heads.

'Then you'd better take this,' he said, unclipping a police walkie-talkie from the back of his belt. 'If you see anything important, press the button marked **PRESS** on the side and talk into it here.' He pointed. 'Okay?'

'Okay,' said Mango and Jilly as Jilly took the walkie-talkie.

'Thanks,' said Flabby Gomez. 'I knew I could rely on you both.'

There was a pelican standing on the roof of the mayor's car. It was Jip, our town mascot. Flabby went over and tucked the bird under his arm. Jip is used to this so didn't complain one bit. 'Well, I must be off to *The Crooked Sixpence*,' Flabby called over. 'Be sure to tell your father what's been happening when he returns.'

'Will do, Mr Mayor!' Mango Claptrap called back.

Chapter Six
Breakout

Now, I suppose I should explain why all the Fox family, including the children, had been in prison (before they escaped, that is). You see, they had all been responsible for a dastardly plot – which I've written about somewhere else, so I'm not going to go to all the time-wasting trouble of repeating it here – but only the parents Derek and Bunty Fox and their eldest child Shaun had received prison sentences. (Judge Mossy Edging is a very fair woman and never accepts bribes unless they're nicely wrapped and come with a hand-written card. And she's never been a fan of locking up children since she saw a film called *Chiddy Chiddy Boom Boom* when she was a girl.) As a result, the three remaining Fox children – Mantle, Fastbuck and Garrideb – had simply been given a stern talking to and told about THE ERROR OF THEIR WAYS.

But, in an effort to stay out of jail and get a big fine or community service instead, Mr and Mrs Fox had argued that the members of their family should ALL stay together. They spent days in court arguing how bad it would be for their children to be separated from them. Judge Mossy Edging finally agreed but, rather than saving them all from jail, she had them ALL put in one big cell.

The Foxes didn't seem to mind prison much. They spent most of their time sitting around discussing how much they hated ducks and how glad they were that there weren't any in their prison cell with them. One of the children – Fastbuck, I think it was – scratched some pictures of ducks on one of the cell walls, and the family spent the following weeks throwing things at them and laughing. They certainly knew how to make their own entertainment.

With all that time on their hands, they even managed to come up with the words for a duck-hating song (to the tune of 'Why've You Got A Chipmunk Down Your Trousers Mistress Herringbone?'):

Ducks are evil.
Ducks are bad.
The thought of ducks
Just drives us mad!
Ducks are evil.
Ducks are bad.
Only dead ducks
Make us glad.
Kill all ducks
Oooo!
Kill all ducks
Doo-bee-doo!

To be fair, it's probably as good as something the Grumbly girls could have come up with, and the Foxes certainly have reasonable singing voices.

But now they'd escaped and there had to be a manhunt – well, a man, woman and children hunt – and, if caught, there'd have to be *another* trial and another prison sentence.

Their method of escape was very straightforward but if I tell you how they did it I might get into trouble. I mean, what if any of you lot end up in jail and escape using the same method? And then you go and get yourself caught and tell the police that you got the idea from a book by Beardy Ardagh spelled A-R-D-A-G-H? I could end up inside a cell myself. So, no thank you very much. Let me just say that the Foxes found a devilishly simple way of getting out of Grubtown Jail, and leave it at that.

What was less smart was bopping Wide Brim Petty-Mandrake over the head and stealing his hearse. First off, even though

Wide Brim Petty-Mandrake was even more unpopular than the Foxes and even though most citizens of Grubtown loved the *idea* of bopping Wide Brim Petty-Mandrake over the head, no one liked escaped prisoners bopping people over the head for real, whoever it was who got bopped. Secondly, if you're going to steal a car for a getaway, it would make sense to choose one that blends in with all the other cars . . . not a hearse which stands out like a penguin at a pink flamingo party.

The hearse was very long and very thin and very black. (Also a bit penguiny.)

At the time it had a rolled-up Persian rug in the back of it (where a coffin would go). This was because Petty-Mandrake had been planning to take the rug back to the shop, or maybe even to Persia – which, according to one of our two local papers,★ is now called Iran – because it either had too many knots in it or not enough. (Apparently the number of knots in

★*The Grubtown Daily Herald* or
The Grubtown Weekly Gerald

a Persian rug is a very important matter.)

The thought about the hearse being a silly getaway vehicle must have eventually occurred to Mr Fox. In next to no time, he had stopped the car and ordered his family to abandon it and to hide out in Grubtown's only cinema, which was closed ('due to staff shortages'). He then took the hand-brake off the hearse and pushed it down the hill so it wouldn't be parked by the cinema (and, therefore, the first building the authorities would search). The only thing it hit on the way down was Mrs Awning's wheelie shopping-basket which, in turn, hit Mrs Awning a glancing blow, sending her head-first into a display of extra-prickly cacti in the 'arid garden' section of the floral display by the Big Man Gomez Memorial Toilets.

Grubtown's cinema is actually called **SMOKY'S** because it stands on the site of some of the old smokehouses where fish used to be smoked. In fact, if you sit through a very long film, such as *Dancing with Whales* or that one about that orphan chicken trying to find its way home, you usually come out smelling faintly of kippers. This is why Hetty Glue-Pen, the manager and projectionist, always leaves a window open and why it was so easy for the Foxes to climb inside. (Hetty also sells the tickets. The only other member of staff was the doorman who wore a very impressive doorman's uniform and mirror dark-glasses apparently to add a touch of glamour to a – smoky – night out at the movies.)

The Fox family sat next to each other in the front row, staring up at the red curtains covering the blank screen.

'What now?' said Mrs Fox.

'We wait,' said Mr Fox.

'I still don't know why we bothered escaping,' said Shaun Fox.

'We were going to be released in two

weeks anyway,' added Garrideb Fox. 'That's when our sentence finishes.'

'*Would* have finished,' Fastbuck Fox corrected him. 'If they capture us, there will be another trial –'

'And a new, longer sentence,' said Mantle Fox.

'QUIET!' said Mr Fox. 'All of you. We should never have been put in prison for what we did. You know full well that we're innocent victims of this evil duck-loving town. Even the town emblem and mascot is a pelican which

is about as near as a bird can get to being a
duck without actually being one!'

'They're sick,' Bunty Fox agreed with her
husband.

The others spat as though they had a nasty
– ducky – taste in their mouths.

'So we have to tell the rest of the world
about our plight!' said Mr Fox.

'Our what?' asked Garrideb, his only
daughter.

'Plight. Predicament. Situation . . . about
the mess we're in through no fault of our

own. This jailbreak will get our unfair treatment the publicity we deserve.'

'You mean in the local papers?'★ asked Fastbuck. Before he'd gone to prison he'd been writing about forty letters a week to them, usually complaining about ducks, but they didn't publish any of them any more.

'Not those *rags*,' snapped his father. 'I mean proper national papers. *Inter*national papers. News of our jailbreak could spread across the globe. It'll be a great chance for us to tell our side of the story!'

'Not if we get arrested first,' said Bunty. 'Do keep your voice down, Derek.'

'Sorry,' he said.

They all stared at the red curtains across the blank screen some more.

★*The Grubtown Daily Herald* and *The Grubtown Weekly Gerald*

Chapter Seven
An Interesting Discovery

Mustard Tripwire was right. Chief Grabby Hanson *had* been going to *The Crooked Sixpence* and now there he was, along with Mayor Gomez and Jip the pelican too. Hanson called for Dr Fraud to check out the bump on Wide Brim Petty-Mandrake's head.

'But he's not a proper doctor!' protested Petty-Mandrake.

'But he's cheap,' said Grabby

Hanson, 'so here's the deal. If you let Dr Fraud take a look at you, the Police Department pays and it won't cost you nothing –'

'Anything,' Petty-Mandrake corrected him (with that REALLY ANNOYING squeaky voice of his).

Grabby Hanson glared at him with his best chief-of-police stare. 'But if you want another doctor to look at that bump, then you pay the bill yourself.'

'Dr Fraud will do just fine, thank you, Chief,' said Petty-Mandrake.

'I thought he might,' said the police chief.

While Grabby asked the undertaker a few questions in Carlo Monte's office, Carlo, Partial Coggs and Purple Outing sat around a card table in the gaming room. (*The Crooked Sixpence* is only open for business in the evenings, remember.) The mayor, meanwhile, fixed a fish-paste sandwich for Jip the pelican in Pageant

Conquest's kitchen area. As soon as he'd pushed the two thick slices of bread together, he tossed it at Jip whose beak flipped open and caught the tasty treat like a hungry pedal-bin. He made a kind of clicking noise to show his appreciation.

Soon after this, Officer Tripwire brought Dr Fraud across in the motor launch to inspect Wide

Brim Petty-Mandrake's bump.

He poked it. He prodded it. He looked at it from all angles.

'It's a bump on the head,' the (pretend) doctor announced at long last.

'Is it serious, Doc?' asked Chief Hanson.

'Well, it certainly made me smile,' said Dr Fraud.

The police chief smiled too.

'This is no laughing matter!' squeaked Petty Mandrake.

'It most certainly is not,' agreed Grabby. 'Those Foxes have gone too far this time.'

Suddenly the police chief's police walkie-talkie crackled to life. '*Grabby? Grabby? Are you there?*' said a voice.

Grabby grabbed the radio from his belt and spoke into it. 'Is that you, Pageant?'

'*Of course it's me,*' said his sister.

'What is it?'

'*Lefty Scorn has spotted the Foxes.*'

'Is he with you?'

'*Yes.*'

'Put him on, will you.'

'*Hello, Chief?*'

'Hello, Lefty. Where are they?'

'*They're in Smoky's. I saw them through the window Hetty Glue-Pen always leaves open –*'

'Do you think they saw you?'

'*I'm pretty sure they didn't,*' said Lefty Scorn, proprietor of Grubtown's laundrette and jewellery store.

'Good work, Lefty,' said Grabby Hanson. 'Keep an eye on the cinema from a safe distance but don't try anything heroic. If they leave just follow them. Don't try to stop them.'

'Sure thing,' said Scorn. It was a slow day at the laundrette and he hadn't sold any jewellery in weeks, so he'd jumped at the chance of being one of the townsfolk playing detective for a day. It wasn't often that you got asked to help keep an eye out for escaped prisoners.

The only reason that I myself wasn't more actively involved in helping to look for the Foxes was that I had a piece to write for a magazine. (Amongst other things, I review famous people's beards and moustaches for **Hairy Faces Monthly**.)

Hanson told Flabby Gomez the latest on the Foxes, then had Mustard Tripwire take them and Constable Gelatine back to dry land.

'What about me? whined Wide Brim Petty-Mandrake.

'Don't try heading any footballs for a while,' said Dr Fraud, snapping shut his very impressive looking doctor's bag.

At the same time that Grubtown's mayor and entire police department were heading for **SMOKY'S** cinema as quickly as they could, Jilly Cheeter was taking another opportunity to have a peek at that uniform. Leaving Mango Claptrap to keep a lookout for escaped duck-haters from the top of the lighthouse, she went all the way down to the entrance hall and opened the built-in wardrobe. It wasn't as if it was in one of Garlic Hamper's *private* rooms, she thought.

She lifted out the uniform on its hanger.

It was deep blue and had an amazing red epaulette on each shoulder fringed with gold brocade.

It had even more fancy gold brocade around the buttons.

And what buttons. They were impossibly shiny. They were *exactly* the way I hope the gold inside a treasure chest will look if I ever dig one up.

There was something strangely familiar about the uniform.

Jilly Cheeter was sure that she'd seen it before.

But where?

Then she saw that there was something else on the floor of the wardrobe. She reached in and lifted out a pair of mirror dark-glasses.

'Cool shades,' said Mango Claptrap leaning over her shoulder.

Jilly's heart jumped. 'What are you doing sneaking up on me?' she asked.

'What are you doing going through the wardrobe?' Mango asked right back.

'Well –'

'And what's Garlic Hamper doing with the doorman's uniform from Smoky's in his . . .?' He fell silent.

It suddenly occurred to both Jilly and Mango that they'd never wondered who the doorman outside the cinema actually was. To them he was just the doorman outside the cinema. They couldn't know *every* grown-up in Grubtown, now, could they?

'You don't think – ?' began Jilly Cheeter.

'– that Garlic Hamper is – ?' continued
Mango Claptrap.

'– the doorman at the cinema – ?' added
Jilly Cheeter.

'– as well as being the lighthouse keeper?'
Mango Claptrap finished.

'But surely that's against the rules?' said
Jilly. 'Isn't the lighthouse keeper supposed to
be in the lighthouse at all times?'

'In case the bulb goes "ping" and a ship
ploughs up the beach, you mean?' asked

Mango.

'Wow!' said Jilly, her eye widening. 'A secret double life!'

'But it's a long way from here to the cinema at the top of Steep Hill,' Mango pointed out, 'and surely he'd have been spotted heading there and back over the years?'

'And why isn't he working at the cinema at the moment?'

'Because,' said Mango Claptrap, who is a one for smart ideas, 'the mayor sent him away while the lighthouse is being mended, so the cinema has had to close *due to staff shortages*.'

'That's enough proof for me!' whooped Jilly.

Chapter Eight
Things Turn Nasty

'We've been rumbled!' shouted Derek Fox, running into the cinema auditorium. He'd just been to the loo and had spotted Flabby Gomez from a window. The mayor had been doing his best to hide behind a litter bin near the water-fountain, but it wasn't big enough for his big, big body. (No litter bin would be.)

'What do we do now?' demanded Bunty Fox.

A nasty duck-hating kind of sneer crossed Mr Fox's already not very nice-looking face. 'We take hostages!' he said triumphantly.

'But we're the only ones here,' said Garrideb, with a sigh which suggested that she didn't always think that daddy-dearest came up with the best of ideas.

'Hostages don't always have to be *people*,' said Mr Fox.

'We're going to take DUCKS hostage?' asked Shaun excitedly.

'I don't see any of them wandering about,' said Fastbuck.

'Follow me,' said their father.

The entire Fox family hurried up the back stairs to the projection room. Along one wall was a series of open wooden shelves stacked high with circular metal film cans. Each of the cans in the largest pile was labelled: *E-P-A-A-B-D* followed by a number, in Hetty Glue-Pen's neat copperplate handwriting, starting with the can labelled *E-P-A-A-B-D 1* at the bottom.

'*These* will be our hostages!' said Derek Fox.

'What are you on about, Dad?' asked Garrideb.

'What does E-P-A-A-B-D mean?' asked Fastbuck.

'These cans contain films of every

Everyone-Parade-About-A-Bit-Day since Flabby Gomez became mayor and came up with the idea,' their dad explained. 'And most of the films are taken up with Gomez himself parading around in his silly curtain robe. He'd be heartbroken if anything happened to these.' He banged the pile of cans with a satisfying clunk. 'Now help me get them downstairs.'

The last thing Grabby Hanson expected was the double doors to **SMOKY'S** being thrown open wide before he'd even had a chance to try to negotiate with the escaped convicts through his police megaphone. But that was exactly what happened.

And there in the doorway stood Mr Derek Fox with a smug look on his face and a pile of film cans (almost as tall as he was) to one side of him.

'Listen to me, Gomez!' he said. 'I have demands and I want them met.'

He was very excited. He'd never imagined that he'd get to insist that his demands were met. Insisting that demands be met was something that tough villains did in films and on TV . . . not (rather unsuccessful) shopkeepers in Grubtown.

'What *are* you talking about, Derek?' Grabby Hanson asked through the megaphone.

'I want the world media here along with a helicopter and –' someone spoke to Derek Fox from inside, out of earshot of the policeman '– and two coffees – white no sugar – a slurp, a Krimson Kola and a glass of milk –' The out-of-earshot voice spoke again, and Derek Fox listened. 'And make sure that's a glass of milk, not a cup or mug. And nice and cold. Okay?'

'*Not* okay!' said Grabby, dropping his arm and letting the megaphone fall to his side. He wandered over to the entrance. 'I'm sorry to be the bringer of bad news, Derek,' he said. 'But I think you're forgetting something rather important.'

'Which is?'

'You don't have any weapons.'

'That's where you're wrong,' said Derek Fox. He opened his hand to show that he'd been clenching his fist around a box of matches he'd found in the ticket office.

'You're going to threaten to smoke yourself to death if we don't get you a helicopter?' said

Flabby Gomez, in disbelief, coming out from behind the bin.

Derek Fox kicked the pile of film cans. They wobbled. The mayor looked at them. 'Films catch alight very easily,' said Mr Fox.

Flabby saw the numbered *E-P-A-A-B-D* labels, written in Hetty Glue-Pen's copperplate handwriting.

He went as white as a very white sheet indeed.

'You wouldn't,' he said.

★ ★ ★

Jilly Cheeter hung the cinema doorman's outfit back inside the wardrobe, placed the cool mirror shades back on the wardrobe floor and shut the door. Mango Claptrap flicked the light switch on the wall to the right.

'This switch has been puzzling me,' he said.

'How so?' asked Jilly.

'Well, there's no bulb down here or on the stairs, so which light is it supposed to switch on where?'

'Perhaps one on the first floor,' Jilly suggested, 'so you don't walk into a dark room when you reach the top of the stairs?'

'Maybe,' said Mango, but he didn't sound convinced. He flicked the switch once more.

'Hey,' said Jilly, 'do that again ... And keep doing it.'

Mango did as he was told. The light switch was an old one: a metal square box with a satisfyingly large bobble-ended switch.

Click. Click. Click. Click.

'Look!' said Jilly. She pointed to the thin gap at the bottom of the wardrobe doors. There was a faint bar of light shining through. She opened the door. The inside of the wardrobe was dimly lit.

She pulled aside the impressive uniform on its lonely hanger. Behind it, set in the wall was another door (painted a stony colour to match the wall). The light – a little brighter – was shining from under that one.

'A secret passage!' gasped Jilly.

'Fantastic!' said Mango.

Jilly Cheeter climbed into the wardrobe and pulled the handle of the inner door. It wouldn't budge. 'We need a key,' she said.

She looked around the inside of the wardrobe. There was no sign of one conveniently hanging on a hook or nail.

Mango checked the outside: the items

hanging on the wardrobe doors. He even checked inside the non-matching wellington boots. Nothing.

Then he had another of his oh-so-splendid ideas. 'Check the pockets of the uniform.'

Jilly slipped her hand inside one pocket and then another. First, her hand closed around on what turned out to be half-eaten packet of extra strong mints, next it closed around what was most definitely a small key. She pulled it out and quickly tried it in the ancient lock. The door opened to reveal a well-lit passage leading through solid rock.

'Shall we?' said Jilly Cheeter.

'Why not!' said Mango Claptrap, clambering into the wardrobe behind her.

Neither Jilly nor Mango had been in a secret passage before but part of them had expected that, if they *did* ever find themselves in one, it would involve a sliding wooden panel and flaming torches on the wall ... Not one entered through the back of a wardrobe and lit by electricity all the way.

'Where do you think it leads?' asked Mango.

'To the cinema, of course,' said Jilly.

'Why "of course"?' asked Mango, marvelling at how much work must have gone into hacking or drilling through all that solid rock.

'Because this must be how Garlic Hamper gets to Smoky's without being spotted!' said Jilly.

'You don't think he built it, do you?' asked Mango, then answered his own question: 'No, that would be impossible and, anyway, everyone would have heard his tunnelling! It would be hard to hide the noise of drilling through solid rock! This passage must have been built at the same time as the lighthouse. Back then, the smokehouses were where the cinema is now.'

'But why?' said Jilly. She had reached some steps cut out of the solid rock and began the steady climb upwards. 'Why should the lighthouse be linked to the smokehouses?'

'Something to do with smuggling?' Mango suggested excitedly.

Of course, what YOU know and I know is that while Jilly Cheeter and Mango Claptrap were merrily making their way along the tunnel towards the cinema, the escaped Fox family were actually holed up in that self-same cinema with their film-can hostages. But Jilly and Mango didn't know that.

Unfortunately.

Chapter Nine
Foxed Again

'The mayor may care about the stupid old films, Derek,' said Bunty Fox, 'but I doubt the police do. How long before they storm the building and throw us all back in jail?'

'Especially now that the angry mob has arrived,' said Shaun, who had lifted the edge of a blackout curtain and was peering through one of the windows at the front.

107

The angry mob actually comes from nearby Werty, except for its self-appointed leader, Farflung Heaps, who has a house not far from mine (but not nearly as nice). Each member owns his or her own flaming torch – not lit all the time, of course – and a pitchfork or big bit of wood, which they can wave about at the first sign of trouble. It's good to stay on the right side of the angry mob (which is usually behind it) and today it was helping the Grubtown Police Department.

'Hmmm,' said Derek Fox. 'Things could turn nasty.' (He was no doubt forgetting that he and his family are probably the nastiest thing in Grubtown.)

Meanwhile, outside, Farflung Heaps had accidentally pressed the button in the drinking fountain with his elbow as he walked past. It squirted him in the face, making him even MORE angry.

'We could always escape down this secret

passage,' Mantle suggested.

'What secret passage?' asked Bunty, his mum.

'The one I've just found behind this fire hose,' said Mantle.

They all turned to look.

On the wall behind Mantle was a big hose, rolled up inside a large bright red metal wheel with the word **FIRE** stencilled on it in white paint. Mantle pulled on the wheel, like you might pull the handle to a giant safe door in the vault of a bank. And, like the door of a giant safe in the vault of a bank, a section of wall swung open behind it to reveal: *the tunnel*.

'Come on!' said Derek Fox and, before you could say sneaky-back-way-out-of-there, he, Bunty, Shaun, Garrideb, Fastbuck and – finally – Mantle had piled into the tunnel and were on their way out of **SMOKY'S**.

'Not fair,' muttered Mantle. 'I should have

gone first.' But he was careful to swing the secret door shut behind him.

I know what you're thinking, so let's pause for a diagram:

Yup, to borrow the title of one of the Grumbly girls' songs: '**There Are Often Surprises Just Around The Corner Even When You Don't Know That There's A Corner (Which Is Another One Of The Surprises)**'.

There were Jilly Cheeter and Mango Claptrap merrily making their way down the tunnel, unaware that a bunch of duck-hating escaped prisoners was heading straight for them. Until . . .

'What was that?' whispered Jilly Cheeter, stopping in her tracks.

'What was what?' asked Mango Claptrap, smart enough to whisper too because Jilly had been.

'I hear voices!'

They listened. Whoever it was in the tunnel was singing. They were singing: '*Kill all ducks/Oooo!/Kill all ducks/Doo-bee-doo!*' to the tune of 'Why've You Got A Chipmunk Down Your Trousers Mistress Herringbone?'.

'THE FOXES!!!' Mango Claptrap and Jilly Cheeter mouthed to each other in absolute (and amazed) silence. They turned and ran back in the direction they'd come.

Spilling out of the wardrobe like the children in that well-known story about children spilling out of a wardrobe, Jilly and

Mango had to think quickly.

'Shall we lock the inner door?' asked Jilly.

'Yes,' said Mango, then: 'No! I've got an idea . . .'

'What is it?' asked Jilly.

'We'll have to be quick!' shouted Mango Claptrap, already throwing open the door to the lighthouse and dashing outside. 'Follow me!'

Jilly Cheeter dashed out after Mango to find him grabbing hold of the tangle of old fishing nets. 'Give me a hand!' he said. 'We've got to get these inside.'

They heaved and they ho-ed and, between them, managed to drag the nets through the doorway and into the hallway.

'If we could get up on top of the wardrobe we could drop the net down on the Foxes when they've all come through,' said Mango.

Jilly shook her head. 'We'll never get ourselves and the nets up there, even if we had a ladder and loads of time. They're too big and too heavy . . .'

'Then let's try spreading them out on the floor,' said Mango Claptrap, urgently.

They'd just managed to spread some of the netting on to the stone floor of the lighthouse hallway in front of the wardrobe when the wardrobe doors flew open and Derek Fox emerged into the light, followed by Bunty, their daughter Garrideb and their sons Shaun, Fastbuck and Mantle. There was a 'crunch' every time one of them stepped on the mirror sunglasses before stepping out of the wardrobe and on to the floor. And the nets.

'Yerch!' said Bunty Fox. 'It's that horrid duck-loving Cheeter girl!'

At which point, that horrid duck-loving Cheeter girl gave the part of the nets on the ground a mighty yank, causing the Foxes to lose their footing and fall to the ground with

various **Ooofs!** and **Ouches!**. She and
Mango Claptrap then threw the rest of the
jumble of nets on top of the Foxes, unravelling
them as they went.

The more the Fox family tried to free
themselves, the more of a tangle they got

themselves into.

Stepping around them, Jilly climbed back into the wardrobe and locked the inner door. She replaced the key in the pocket of the uniform. She then closed the outer doors. Mango, meanwhile, flicked the light switch.

He unclipped the police walkie-talkie from the belt of his funny shorts. (Jilly Cheeter wasn't wearing a belt to clip it to.) 'Calling Chief Hanson! Calling Chief Hanson! Are you receiving me, over?' he asked.

'*Receiving you loud and clear,*' Grabby replied. '*Who is that, over?*'

'It's Mango Claptrap and Jilly Cheeter,' said Mango. 'And we've captured your escaped prisoners. Every one of them!'

It didn't take long for things to get back to normal. The Foxes were back behind bars with Mickey 'Steamroller' Johnson in next to no time. (So far they still don't know that he was the one who tipped off the mayor about their planned escape. I only found this out myself on Wednesday.)

Within a matter of weeks the lighthouse was up and running again, with Garlic Hamper back at his post with his matchstick models all around him. No thanks to Mango's dad of course. In the end the mayor had needed to call in a proper electrician. (Furl Claptrap did manage to get the old light bulb down in one piece, though, and it's now in our local museum.)

The Plucked Grape was refloated and then sold for scrap, so Vestige Claptrap and his fellow stone-throwers have gone back to using those notices of Grabby Hanson's as targets. THE RUSTY DOLPHIN hasn't been rebuilt yet, but that's only a matter of time.

Flabby Gomez was still busy knitting his family's dream home. And, while I remember, Tundra Gomez – his idiot son in the cowboy suit – got a job with a different kind of outfit. He's now the doorboy at **SMOKY'S** cinema (except for the late-night showings twice a week when a guy called Limbo Goulash does the job after he's finished at the office). Apparently, the original doorman retired. No questions asked.

As for Wide Brim Petty-Mandrake, the bump on his head soon went down, he got his money back on that Persian rug I told you about AND he's just started a petition to try to ban all talking after 9 p.m.

Anywhere.

Jilly Cheeter and Mango Claptrap can now add another medal each to their collection (even bigger and shinier than the last). The mayor held an open-air medal-giving ceremony outside the lighthouse and had a new hat made especially for the occasion. He had the whole thing filmed by

Hetty Glue-Pen for the town archives. Unfortunately, someone stole the camera but Chief Grabby Hanson knows exactly who that was and plans to make an arrest sometime soon.

The day ended with the release of a whole new flock of ducks into Grubtown. I think this was done to annoy the Fox family more than anything else, which was a great idea. But who needs ceremonies anyway? We citizens of Grubtown will *always* remember the far from great escape.

THE END

Another word from Beardy Ardagh

Whentell people about events in Grubtown, they usually ask why so many of the townsfolk 'have such silly names'. I'll bet they think that they're the first person to have asked me that. Well, if you're one of those people, then I've got news for you. I'm not only SICK AND TIRED of the question, I also think that YOUR name is silly, and I don't even know what it is.

Anyway, what's so silly about the Grubtowners' names?

There used to be a British politician called Manny Shinwell and nobody threw rocks at him and shouted, 'Silly name! Silly name!' And, if they had, he probably would have had the last laugh because he became a lord and lived to be a hundred-and-one, while the name-callers would probably have curled up and died in their damp caves before they were fifty. So there.

If, for some ridiculous reason, you'd like to write to me about **Grubtown Tales**, please address the envelope:

Beardy Ardagh,
c/o Faber & Faber,
Bloomsbury House
74–77 Great Russell Street,
London,
WC1B 3DA

and write **Grubtown Tales** in the bottom left-hand corner. DON'T FORGET TO INCLUDE A STAMPED SELF-ADDRESSED ENVELOPE if you're hoping for a reply. (If I had to buy all the stamps and envelopes myself, I'd probably have to end up drinking water from dirty puddles to save money.) Not that I can promise you'll get a reply, of course. I may soak off the stamp and use it to send a letter to someone else.

(Just some of) the folk who pop up in GRuBtoWN taLes

Jilly Cheeter girl and one-time duck-gatherer

Mango Claptrap a short boy in short trousers, whatever the weather

Manual Org a smoothy skinned fellow

Flabby Gomez Mayor of Grubtown

Kumquat 'Grabby' Hanson the chief of police

The Grumbly girls the seven Grumbly daughters

Hacking-Cough Gomez the mayor's brother

Big Man Gomez the mayor's dead dad

Pritt Gomez the mayor's wife

Tundra Gomez the mayor's son and heir

Formal Dripping official village idiot for the
nearby village of Werty

**Derek, Bunty, Shaun, Mantle, Fastbuck &
Garrideb Fox** the duck-hating Fox family of
humans (not foxes)

Rambo Sanskrit council job-giver-outer

Sonia Pipkin local builder

The troll inhabitant of Beardy Ardagh's airing
cupboard

Mrs Awning town accident-waiting-to-happen,
first name unknown

Minty Glibb owner of Minty's Cake Shop

Mickey 'Steamroller' Johnson doughnut-
loving steamroller driver

Leggy Prune the future Mrs Johnson

Mrs Johnson the former Leggy Prune

Constable Gelatine a police sergeant

Mustard Tripwire an officer of the law and
Gelatine's nephew

Galaxy Tripwire a train driver and former
beauty queen

Relish Tripwire a tropical fish salesperson

Informative Boothe a very knowledgeable chap

Hobo Browne a gentleman of the road/smelly
tramp

Camshaft Thrift owner of The Rusty Dolphin
Cafe

Farflung Heaps self-appointed leader of an
angry mob

Garlic Hamper the lighthouse keeper

Shoona Loose the world-famous singer who
does a lot for animal charities

Tawdry Hipbone movie star

Snooks Miss Hipbone's pampered pooch

Luminous Shard bald heckler and mechanic

Carlo Monte the riverboat gambler

Lefty Scorn proprietor of Scorn's Laundrette
& Jeweller's

Acrid Scorn an irresponsible dumper of
hazardous waste

Jip the town pelican (official mascot)

Marley Gripe a painter of signs

Dr Fraud a pretend doctor (but he's cheap)

Sloop Cheeter Jilly's dad

Harvey the Cheeter family dog

Furl Claptrap Mango's dad

Carport Claptrap Mango's mum

Vestige Claptrap Mango's brother

Claws their cat

Partial Coggs Grubtown's resident artist

Slackjaw Gumshoe paint & hardware store
owner

Purple Outing very rich owner of Purple
Outing's Music Shack

Hind-Leg Outing amongst other things,
mother of Purple's vast number of children

Wide Brim Petty-Mandrake a regular
complainer

Hetty Glue-Pen cinema manager and
projectionist

Condo Blotch former cleaner now head of her
very own keep-fit and health-food empire

Emily Blotch Condo's daughter

Free-Kick leader of the escaped lab rats

Lulu Free-Kick's mate for life

Hardfast Tendril Grubtown's chief forester

Paltry Feedback a printer and cake
decorator

Careworn Wormwood nine-day king of Grubtown

Glowering Silt general manager of Fettle's hotel

Avid Folklore manager of Fettle's hotel

Chevvy Offal owner of Offal's Sunbeds

Premix Stipend victim of one of Offal's sunbeds

Pageant Conquest food-maker (and Grabby Hanson's sister)

Mossy Edging a very fair judge who doesn't take bribes *that* often

Hybrid Byword the (now dead) TV chef

Limbo Goulash an office worker

Clam Wretching founder of Wretching's Dairy

Barton Wretching her son and current owner of the dairy

Beardy Ardagh honoured citizen of Grubtown and the teller of these tales

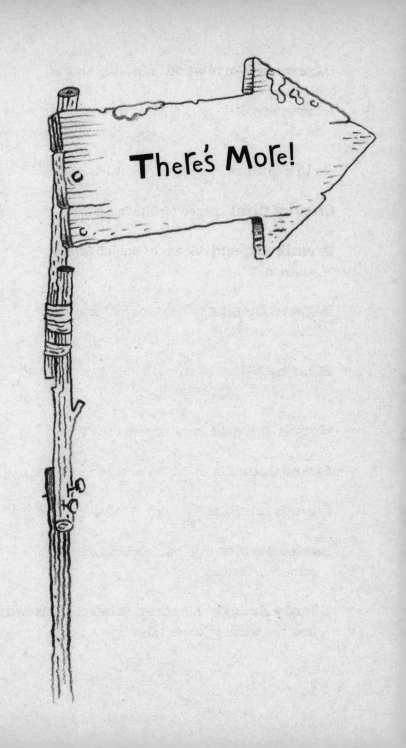

The delightful Beardy Ardagh tells of other GRuBtoWN taLes

Here's the deal. I tell you about some of the other **GRuBtoWN taLes** and you promise to make sure that every home in the country (and most of the towns) has a copy. You give **GRuBtoWN taLes** as gifts. You ask for **GRuBtoWN taLes** as gifts in return. You mention **GRuBtoWN taLes** in conversations (even in your sleep) and you write about them every time you're near a mobile phone, computer, pencil, pen, piece of charcoal or anything else that you can write with. Deal? Good. Then read on . . .

Look out for

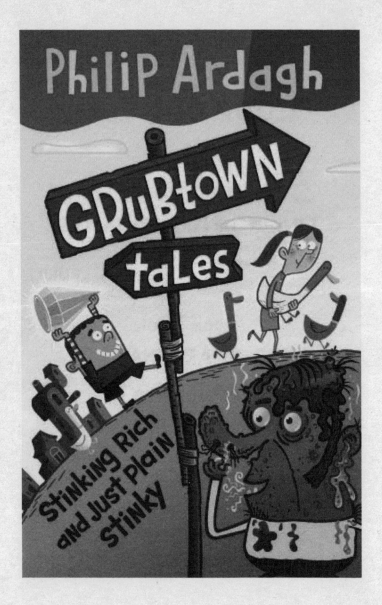

GRuBtoWN tales

Book One

Stinking Rich aNd Just PlaiN StiNky

Grubtown is full of oddballs – from the singing Grumbly girls to a family of duck-haters, and an outsized mayor who's knitting a new house – but Manual Org is too repulsive even for them. Getting him to leave town is top priority, until the discovery of a humongous diamond changes everything.

**YOU SHOULD HAVE READ
THIS ONE ALREADY!**

GRuBtoWN tales
Book Two

The YeaR That It RaiNed Cows

A startled cow falling out of nowhere on to Limbo Goulash while he's riding Marley Gripe's bicycle marks the start of a chain of events strange even by Grubtown's standards. Soon damaged property includes Purple Outing's Music Shack and Minty Glibb's attempt at the world's largest (strawberry) jelly-trifle. With Mayor Flabby Gomez throwing a wobbly, all chief of police, Grabby Hanson, can do is have the cow-fearing townsfolk watch the skies. Underground, meanwhile, there lies another big surprise.

YOU SHOULD HAVE READ THIS ONE TOO!

Nearly there!

'Bye!'